I0624242

ENDANGERED SPECIES

Edward M. Grant

Banchixi Media
Canada

First Edition, 2014

Paperback
ISBN-13: 978-1-927549-21-6

eBook
ISBN-13: 978-1-927549-20-9

Published by Banchixi Media, **www.banchixi.com**

ENDANGERED SPECIES

"Get off your fat ass and find yourself a job," Felicia yelled across the fifty metre wide living room of her parents' mansion.

Dirk Beretta was slumped on the sofa, eating nachos and watching the latest reality XP show following the Phat City cheerleaders. He was about to tell her his ass wasn't fat, it was just muscular from years of Space Marine training and genetic enhancement, when he realized that a month of all the nachos he could eat, and all the XP broadcasts he could watch, had not been good for him. If he didn't exercise those muscles soon, he would be a mass of flab.

Which was why, two weeks later, he was sitting on a cheap sofa outside an office at the top of the tower of the mining ship *Pooper-Scooper* on the Platypus Planet, as the new security chief for the BastadoCorp mining operation. He had scoured the Galactic network for employment ads, and it was the first job which seemed to suit his particular skills.

His skulltop computer beeped, for at least the tenth time that day. He'd considered turning it off, but that would only get him into even more trouble.

Are you missing me yet? Or are you dead? I need to know.

After sending him to work ten thousand light years away, Felicia was now sending messages every fifteen minutes, asking how it was going, and how much he missed her.

It's almost enough to make a man turn to drink, he thought as he knocked back a can of beer. His first meeting with his new boss was more important than sending love letters.

Vaulted windows ran from floor to ceiling on the outer hull of the ship, and, through them, he could see the rough dirt far below where the Destructobots had torn up the lush jungle outside. In the distance trees fell as Destructobots tore them down, ready for Minerbots to rip up the soil and extract whatever was beneath. He didn't know what they were mining for, and really didn't care so long as the job gave him some peace and quiet away from Felicia's nagging.

The PA sat at her desk by the window, and brushed her long brown hair away from her eyes. From the fur, whiskers and tail Dirk guessed she was half chipmunk. BastadoCorp was a multi-planetary corporation with mines across half the galaxy, yet this was the first time since he arrived that Dirk had seen a non-human employee.

She looked up at him and smiled.

Dirk winked back at her. He preferred girls who shaved, but years of combat in the Space Marines had taught him that you can't be too choosy when you're thousands of light years from home. She reminded him of his old girlfriend, Sergeant Vixen, except the PA was fluttering her eyelids at him, not rotting in a grave at Din Bin Foo.

A light on her desk buzzed. She looked at the clock on the wall, stood and wobbled across the room on her stiletto heels. A drink replicator stood on a table between two miniature palm trees in pots. She punched a button on the replicator and a steaming cappuccino emerged from the slot at the bottom. Then she adjusted her short skirt and tail, picked up the cup and carried it into the office. Dirk sat back to wait.

A few moments later the door opened and she walked out, lipstick smeared, adjusting her blouse.

"Mr Bastado will see you now," she squeaked.

She sat at her desk and pulled her lipstick from her purse, then began to tidy up the smears. Dirk knocked on the door, then stepped into the office.

Mr Bastado was slumped behind a glass desk in an enormous chair, the flab at his sides drooping over the arms. The chair floated above the floor, wobbling gently in an anti-grav field, most likely because no chair legs known to man could have supported the weight.

A lizard sat on his knee, its tongue flicking in and out of its mouth as Bastado stroked its back. Something about the man disturbed Dirk, but he didn't quite know how to put it.

"You're not wearing any pants," he said.

The anti-grav generator creaked as Bastado leaned back in his chair. "Is that a security problem?"

Was a lack of pants a security problem? Dirk thought for a moment, but finally concluded that he couldn't really see any way it could be, except to the parts Bastado would normally keep there. He shook his head.

"Good. Because you are my security chief, and anything that's not a security problem is none of your business. I didn't build this company from my first shovel in my parents' back yard so some dumb ex-Marine could tell me whether I should wear pants."

Dirk nodded. It made sense.

Bastado lit a cigar and pointed the burning end toward Dirk. "I run this company, and I run it how I want, when I want. Many people who disagreed with me have had accidents with grinding machines. Do you understand?"

Dirk nodded again, though he wished those details had been included in the contract when he took the job. All Bastado had mentioned were free guns, free beer, and being thousands of light years away from his girlfriend.

Bastado tried to stand, but his thin, short arms could not lift his weight from the chair. After several failed attempts, he slumped back and held out his hand. Dirk leaned over the desk and shook it.

"Good luck, Mr Beretta. Oh, and don't get any ideas about Floozy out there. When I hire a fur-bag, it's not for her brains." He leaned forward. "And many men I hired who got the hots for fur-bags have had accidents with grinding machines."

"I didn't do anything."

Bastado smirked. "You thought about her. I told her to smile at you and see how you reacted."

"I've got a girl back home..."

"I don't want to have to hire another security chief next week because your balls got caught in the grinding wheels." He waved Dirk away. "Now, go and do your job."

The windows rattled, and a dull thud shook the floor. A cloud of smoke rose into the sky in the distance outside the windows, where a Destructobot was burning at the edge of the jungle.

Bastado pointed his cigar at the window. "And *that* is your job. Either you protect the mine from these trouble-making primitive hippies, or we will drop Nova bombs on the jungle until nothing can attack us again."

Dirk stood at the tree line. The charred, smoking remains of the Destructobot towered above him. Some of the engineers worked on the wreckage in protective suits, removing parts that might still be useful. The whole area smelled of burned rubber, oil and... something worse.

"Anyone see what happened?" he said.

A burly engineer, with a face covered in oil and a name-tag on his suit that said Blair, looked up from the electronics box he was removing from the side of the machine.

He pointed toward a smear of red goo on the grass. "What do you think happened?"

Dirk looked closer. Chunks of fur and bone were scattered throughout the goo. Now he knew what smelled so bad. He'd expected that the first time he saw a platypoid, he'd be looking at their outsides, not their insides.

"God-damn fur-bags attacked the bot," Blair said. "Two of them went in the air intakes and trashed the turbines."

Dirk had fought before in what had been considered suicide attacks, but throwing themselves into the turbines was extreme.

"They sacrificed themselves to destroy the Destructobot?"

Blair cackled. "Not likely. Dumb swamp-rats were trying to stab it with spears, and they got sucked in. You should see their faces on the surveillance tapes. It's a classic."

"What's their problem?"

"They've been pissed ever since we started mining here. This is the third Destructobot we've lost this month."

"Can't anyone stop them?"

"The boss is too busy slipping the sausage to that piece of fur he keeps upstairs, and the last security chief got carried off in a fur-bag attack. Why do you think you're here?"

Dirk had assumed that people were hired and fired all the time on a job like this one. No-one wanted to be stuck in a place like this for years, even if the beer was free. They hadn't mentioned that he might be kidnapped.

He walked closer to the Destructobot and looked up at the wreckage. It looked like a grav tank someone had hit with a Nova bomb. "I thought the platypoids were a peaceful race? And BastadoCorp had bought the mining rights?"

Blair huffed. "They spout all that peace and love shit for the XP shows when they're looking for support, but when they get pissed off it all goes out the window. I've been here a year and we've lost fifty-seven men. Fifty-eight, if the security chief doesn't come back."

Dirk turned to Blair. "The platypoids killed them?"

"Well, twenty-six had accidents with the grinding machine. But the rest, yeah, dead or missing in platypoid attacks. So what are you going to do about it?"

"I should meet the platypoid leaders and see what their grievances are, maybe we can figure something out."

Blair laughed. "What do you think the last security chief was trying to do when he disappeared? The only good fur-bag is a dead fur-bag."

A second engineer turned to them. "But, if they were to stop destroying the Destructobots, we'd be out of a job."

Blair threw an oily bolt at him. "I'd rather be spending my severance pay than getting my balls chopped off by some hippy fur-bag. Kill 'em all."

A buzzer sounded in Dirk's head as he sat at the poolside bar on the third level of the *Pooper-Scooper*. Bambi had sent an email to say she was passing on the way to a swimming competition, and the swim team would stop by to visit, if they could sneak through the quarantine zone to reach the planet. No ship was supposed to come within a hundred light years of a primitive culture without permission, and Bastado was only there because he'd paid for the right to do so. Dirk told her he'd look forward to seeing her, and hoped he wouldn't regret it.

Bastado was a real cheap-skate. The mines had too few guards, and too many Destructobots, so they couldn't guard them all the time. He would send the guards he had on random patrols, and the drones further from the mine to look for platypoids sneaking in to attack. Replacing the broken cameras and microphones on any likely trails would help with advance warning, if he could get Bastado to pay for them. Spears wouldn't offer much of a threat to guards with gauss rifles, and hopefully they could chase the platypoids away without killing any and making things worse.

That was assuming that they were even responsible. For all he knew, the engineers were stuffing platypoids in the air vents so they could work more overtime.

He pulled the video from the surveillance system. A dozen platypoids ran screaming from the jungle, and threw spears at the Destructobot, which ignored the attack because the spears had no effect on its systems. It rolled onward, knocking down everything in its path, and, as the platypoids tried to run away, two tripped and fell. The Destructobot ran right over them, sucking them into the vents.

A dozen engineers in shorts and swimming trunks lounged at the other tables around the pool, chatting and drinking. Dirk slumped back on a lounge chair in the sun, and flipped through reports of previous attacks on Destructobots to see whether he could find any patterns. Floozie swam in the pool, splashing water as she flung her arms around. Her gaze met his as she turned, then she swam toward him.

As she reached the edge of the pool, she stood, revealing the tiny bikini that struggled to control her breasts. She wiped the water from her eyes and climbed out, walked to a nearby lounge chair covered with a pink towel, and stopped beside it to shake her head and body.

Her fur flew out as she shook, and water sprayed the chair and floor. Dirk watched the bikini as it strained to keep her body under control as she jiggled her butt and breasts, the straps stretching and the cloth tightening against her skin. He glanced toward the engineers. They resolutely ignored the show.

Floozie rubbed herself with the towel, then pulled on a pair of sunglasses and lay the towel back on the chair.

Dirk held up a pitcher of beer. "Buy you a drink?"

The engineers' eyes turned toward him. As they saw him look back, they turned away and muttered to each other.

Floozie pulled her sunglasses down her nose. "You know, none of the others have ever risked talking to me. They're afraid of what Mr Bastado might think."

"Dirk Beretta is afraid of no man."

She raised the sunglasses and lay down on her chair. "You could pour me one, but it's all on the house anyway. There aren't many people who'd want to be sober for a year on a BastadoCorp posting."

He poured her a glass and walked over. "Floozy, huh?"

She nodded.

"Nice name," he said.

"With an -ie. Mr Bastado spells it with a -y, and I hate that."

"I'll remember in future."

"Mother always wanted me to go into PA work. She said a memorable name would give me a leg up over the other girls."

Dirk looked at her tiny bikini. "I'm sure it's done that."

He handed her the glass.

"What do you know about these platypoid attacks?"

Floozie glanced around the pool. "Me? Nothing. Why would I know anything about platypoid attacks?"

"You've been here longer than I have. How long is that anyway?"

"I came here with Mr Bastado last month when he flew in to investigate the problems at the mine. But I've never met any of the natives." She scratched her cleavage. "He would never let me, he says I might get fleas."

"So they've been attacking the mine for a while?"

Floozie nodded. "About a year, I gather. What do you think will happen? Mr Bastado talks about bombing them all. That would be horrible."

"I don't think we'll need to go that far."

"You wouldn't really kill them, would you?"

"I wouldn't want to, but I'm sure he would."

She sat up and stretched her shoulders. Her furry cleavage widened and pointed at his face. She leaned toward him.

"But we shouldn't be seen talking to each other," she whispered. "Mr Bastado doesn't like to see any other man show interest in his little chipmunk."

"Is this another of your tests?"

She leaned closer. "Would you care?"

"Why don't we go somewhere more private?"

Floozie purred in the bed alongside Dirk and stretched as she rolled over.

"It's getting late. I have to clean up and put on something frilly for Mr Bastado."

Dirk stretched and wriggled his joints. He was still out of shape, and she had exercised muscles he hadn't used in months. "I should be getting some sleep. I have a busy day tomorrow."

"What are you going to do?"

"After I revise the patrol schedules and check the sensors I'm going to take a walk in the jungle. If I can find the platypoids who are attacking the Destructobots, perhaps we can come to some agreement that would make everyone happy."

"And if you can't?"

"Then I'll suggest to Mr Bastado that we bring in some more guards so we can cover the Destructobots at all times."

"I don't think that's going to work."

"Then he's going to want to bomb them. I have to find something that will stop them doing more damage, so he doesn't go that far."

"Couldn't you just suggest that he leaves them alone? It is their planet, and we are the ones tearing it up."

Dirk shrugged. "Bastado has the paperwork, the platypoids are just backward primitives."

"How do you know they're primitives?"

"They live in the jungle and attack giant robots with spears rather than missiles. That's primitive in my book."

"But that doesn't justify killing them."

"No. Which is why I have to find a way to justify not killing them."

"And if you don't? I wouldn't like it if you decided to do anything bad to them."

"I hope it doesn't come to that."

Floozie threw back the covers and rolled naked on the bed. "Mr Bastado would be very unhappy with you if he found out what you just did to me."

"You were the one who picked me up."

She stroked his chest. "Oh, but he wouldn't believe that, would he? He is so very possessive and so very jealous... just one slip of my tongue, and you'll be on your way to the grinding machines."

She leaned on her elbow, and Dirk watched her breasts wobble as she moved.

She coughed. "I said, one slip of my tongue and you'll be on your way to the grinding machines."

Dirk swung his laser machete to hack a path through the giant ferns at the base of the trees around the wrecked Destructobot. Behind him the engineers were completing the work begun the previous day, removing the last of the useful components and returning them to the ship for repair. They had assembled one Destructobot out of the remains of three wrecked units, and it was now rolling out into the jungle to tear down more trees.

If he worked through the jungle around the *Pooper-Scooper* in a circle, sooner or later he had to run into some evidence of how the platypoids had attacked the Destructobot. They couldn't get close enough to attack it without leaving a trail that would indicate where they came from.

So far, he had found nothing. After an hour, he realized that he didn't know anything about the platypoid people and how they lived, beyond what Bastado, Blair and Floozie had said. Which didn't help, as they had completely different opinions.

He wasn't taking any chances after his past few adventures. He'd borrowed light power armour and a gauss rifle from the armoury, which would be more than enough to handle a few primitives with spears. In hindsight, that hadn't been his best idea, because the humidity was causing havoc in the armour's circuitry. The HUD flickered on and off on the visor, and the air conditioning was blowing hot air as often as cold. He tried to step forward through the gap he'd hacked, but the right leg of the armour wouldn't move. He reached down and slapped it, and it juddered as it took a step forward. He was going to have a long talk with Maintenance when he returned to the mine.

Leaves moved to his left. He dropped to one knee, raised the rifle and peered into the jungle. The leaves blocked the suit's IR sensors, and the radar couldn't see beyond the trees. A snake slithered down a nearby tree trunk and hissed at him.

The leaves moved again to his right. He swung the rifle that way just in time to see a small furry nose and whiskers peer out of a gap between the ferns. A six-legged blob of green fur the size of a poodle padded out and looked up at him. It chirped, then raised a leg and peed on his boot.

Water was running up ahead, and Dirk hacked through ferns to the edge of a large stream. He looked along the bank for any sign of footprints, as it could be an ideal way for a group to sneak through the jungle, if they didn't just swim all the way. Seeing nothing, he looked down at the water. It was moving rapidly away from the mine, but didn't look very deep, so he stepped down into it. The water rose nearly to his waist, but the sealed armour kept his legs dry.

He struggled toward the far bank, hoping he would get there before the legs froze up again. Four steps to go, three steps, two...

Then the right leg stopped moving.

Dirk leaned forward against the straps that held him in the suit. and tightened his thigh muscles. The leg motors groaned and whined, then went silent. He smelled something burning, and a stream of smoke rose from the leg. He coughed as it filled the suit's helmet, until he could no longer see out of the face plate. He flipped it open and felt a blast of warm, wet air on his skin as the smoke began to dissipate. He leaned his weight on the right leg, and swung the left leg toward the shore. Then he tried to pull the frozen leg beside it.

The foot rose from the mud, then the left leg twisted. Before Dirk could react, the suit fell forward and smacked down onto the river bank. His view went dark as the helmet slammed into the mud with a loud squelch.

He reached out, slapped his hands down into the mud, and pushed against the ground with power-assisted muscles until he rolled the suit onto its back. He sighed, and commanded the front of the suit to open, unclipped the straps from his chest and groin, then climbed out.

Piece of crap, he thought as he stood and looked down at the charred and blackened access panel on the hip joint. He crouched and unclipped the panel. Smoke billowed from the interior, and the stench of burned plastic fought with that of rotten vegetation in the jungle. He turned his face away as he waited for the worst of the smell to dissipate, then waved his hand to waft away the rest.

He looked into the hatch. The motor was blackened and burned, and the power cables melted. The suit wasn't walking anywhere by itself again until it had a major service. It was probably war-surplus from decades ago. Bastado clearly didn't cut any corners in his quest to keep costs down.

He heard the swish of something moving through the bushes behind him. He glanced around just in time to see something long and dark swing toward his face.

He opened his mouth to shout for help, and was about to raise his hands to block the blow and make his attacker wish they'd stayed in bed that morning, but was distracted by a pair of furry globes wrapped in leather jiggling toward him.

Nice hooters.

Before he could make a sound, something smashed into the side of his head. He fell from the river bank, his face went under the surface, and his mouth filled with water.

Then everything went dark.

"Feed the dishes! Wash the lawn! Mow the horse!" Felicia shouted. Her face glowed red, and horns sprouted from her perfectly controlled blond hair.

Dirk was relieved to discover she was just a dream, but some days he really wished that he'd let the Space Weasels eat her. He also wished that when the Space Marines had enhanced his body for combat, they'd given him a thicker skull. A dull pain entered his dream from the back of his head.

As he returned to consciousness, he felt water dripping onto his face, and heard chittering jungle animals and the roar of rushing water. He opened his eyes.

He was tied to a rock in a river near the base of a waterfall and on each side of him stood a platypoid girl in a leather bikini with a spear in her hand. He tried to request help through his skulltop computer, but he couldn't get a wireless connection to the mine. They must have carried him out of range.

He raised his head as high as he could with the ropes tied around his shoulders. More platypoid girls stood in the water, or sat on rocks around him.

"Hi," he said.

One of the girls with spears leaned over, giggled, and slapped his face. "Silence, hairless scum."

"My name is Dirk. I want to meet your leaders and see if we can come to some arrangement about the..."

The other girl slapped his face with a hairy paw. Her claws scratched his cheek. "Silence. Our leader approaches."

Dirk lifted his head again, expecting a grizzled platypoid with the scars of war on his face. Instead, he saw a platypoid girl swim toward the rock and rise from the water beside him.

Her lips moved, but Dirk didn't hear the words. He just stared at her, unable to move his eyes. She was furry, and had a bill, and a tail, and wouldn't normally be his kind of girl. But the leather bikini top could barely manage to hold in two of the most perfect breasts he had ever seen.

"I said, do you understand?" she said.

"Sorry, I think I missed something," Dirk said.

She slapped his face. "Your people are raping our planet of its life blood. You will stop or we will kill you all."

"I don't think that's gonna work."

She put her paws on her hips and thrust her chest forward. "Humans are made stupid by greed. Look at you. You come here to protect your men from us, and are captured by two maiden pups."

The platypoid girls giggled.

"That was deliberate," Dirk lied. "I wanted to meet you to talk to you about our problems."

"We have talked enough. You will leave our planet or we will force you from it. That is the only choice we offer you."

"I don't think they're going to agree to that. And they bought the mining rights, so if you try to stop them they'll eventually start killing you." Dirk stared at her cleavage. "And I wouldn't want that to happen, would you?"

"You are more of foolish than I imagined. Humans have no idea whose territory they have invaded. You are pitiful and your threats are empty."

Dirk looked at the platypoid crowd watching them. "If they drop Nova bombs on the jungle, you won't even have time to regret your decision before you're just ash and vapour."

"They would not dare."

Dirk tried to shrug but the ropes prevented him. "As far as they're concerned, this is worthless jungle and you're just an annoyance. If they have to turn it into a hundred mile wide crater before they dig it out, they won't lose any sleep."

She pointed at the platypoid girl guards, then at Dirk. "Kill him."

Dirk opened his mouth to speak, as the girls raised their spears above their heads.

"No, wait!"

The high-pitched shout came from the jungle, and Dirk twisted his head toward it. Floozie waded into the water from the tree line, wearing a thousand dollar leather bikini that Dirk recognized from one of the exotic lingerie catalogues he kept in Felicia's bathroom. It was engineered to expose as much flesh as possible, with cute red hearts showing where to pull the bows to strip it off in seconds.

It suited her.

The spears hovered above his chest. He grit his teeth and heaved against the ropes, but they just creaked, and scraped against the rock. The platypoid leader turned toward Floozie.

"You will not interfere with my decisions."

"Listen to me," Floozie said. "He is not like the others. They were ready to kill you all, just so they could spend their time drinking free beer in the bar. He really does want to find a compromise between both sides."

"Humans lie. They always lie. They promised us peace, then stole our land."

Dirk looked at the platypoid girls, who still held their spears above him. He winked at them. They giggled and winked back. If he wasn't tied up, they wouldn't be maidens for long. Or perhaps tying up their men was how platypoid maidens lost their maidenhood. He was going to have to ask them, when he got a chance.

Floozie trudged through the water to the rock. "He is as close to an honest man as you'll ever find working for Bastado. Listen to what he has to say, or the next security chief will drop bombs on you."

Dirk twisted his wrists against the ropes that held him down. "She's right. If you don't work something out with me, even if Bastado doesn't bomb you, the next guy won't be so eager to help."

He tried to think of happy fluffy bunnies bouncing through the jungle. If he could concentrate his chi power, he would be able to break the ropes before the platypoid girls could stab him. But his thoughts kept wandering to images of the platypoid leader, naked and wet on the beach.

Dirk walked along the riverbank. The platypoid leader had agreed to let him talk to her people, but she wasn't letting him go free. His hands were still tied, and Floozie lead him by a rope around his neck. The two platypoid girls followed behind, giggling and prodding his butt with their spears. He glanced at them, and Floozie pulled on the rope until he turned back.

"Won't Bastado notice you're gone?" he said.

"He's having his afternoon siesta," Floozie said. "And it will be a long one, after the workout I gave him at lunch."

"So you're working for the bad guys?"

"I'm not really a PA. I'm studying Xenobiology, and this was the only way I could get into the quarantine zone to study the platypoid people. Then, when I realized what he was doing, I had to stay to work against him. You've seen how Bastado treats non-humans. He hates these people, and would love an excuse to wipe them out."

"If they'd stop attacking him, he wouldn't be able to justify bombing them."

"They won't do that. Their planet is sacred to them, and they are honour-bound to protect it from him."

"Then why did they sign over the mining rights?"

"Some politician ten thousand miles away signed in return for a box of Altarian sea-shells. These people weren't consulted about it."

"So we're here illegally?"

"Bastado says it's legal, because the world leader signed the paper. But the world leader is just some fat platypoid he pulled out of the river and built a big castle for."

"Next time I go looking for a job, I'm going to be sure to ask some serious questions in the interview."

Dirk looked ahead. The platypoid leader's ass swung as she moved, the motion accentuated by the movement of her tail.

"Who's this platypoid chick anyway?"

"That's Princess Pokaplatus. Her father was the tribe's leader before he was wounded in one of the early attacks on the mine. Bastado caught him, and threw him in the grinding wheels. Her father wanted his son to take over, but he was so useless that she did instead."

"I'd really like to get to know her better."

Floozie pulled on the rope until it scraped against his neck. "Don't even think about it. She's promised to the son of the most powerful family in the tribe. They need a new king, and her brother isn't up to the job."

Dirk clasped his hands together and flexed his muscles. "So if I bone her I could be King Of The Platypoids?"

Floozie shook her head. "Men..."

"Don't platypoids lay eggs?" Dirk said.

"Uh-huh."

"So why do they have... you know?"

"Human sexual characteristics? They are a very interesting species. I believe they are the descendants of the original human colonists living here millenia ago, during the Velan Empire. I think they genetically engineered themselves, to better survive here after the Empire collapsed and stranded them. If I can prove that, it would be worth all the time I've spent here."

"Can I ask you a personal question?"

Floozie looked at him and fluttered her eyelids.

"How do you and Bastado...?"

"Paw clamps on his desk and chair. That is all I'm willing to say."

Dirk tried hard not to imagine the sight of her clamped to Bastado's desk, and almost completely failed. He wondered whether she squeaked for Bastado the way she had for him.

"We're here," Floozie said. "And yes, I fake it for him very well."

Dirk looked up, and saw a crowd of platypoids on rocks around a pool in the jungle. Poka-whatever swam to a rock in the centre of the pool and stood on it. Dirk appreciated the way the water ran down her cleavage.

"Anyway, it's nearly three o'clock," Floozie said. "So I have to get back."

"What happens at three o'clock?"

"Bastado's daily cappucino and blowjob. My knees are killing me. Good luck, and remember you don't have a chance with Pokaplatus."

"I still have to try. If I can get into her pants, maybe I can talk her into working something out with Bastado."

Floozie glared at him for a second, then turned to walk away. Dirk grabbed her shoulder. "Hey, about yesterday. That was just because you wanted to pump some information out of me, right?"

"Yes!" she yelled, and stormed off into the jungle.

Dirk watched her go for a moment, then the platypoid girls prodded him with their spears, and pushed him onward to the pool. He stepped into the water, unsure of what they expected him to do, then Pokaplatus spoke.

"This human wishes to talk to the council."

The platypoids on the rocks gibbered among themselves. Then one of the males stood.

"We do not talk to humans. Humans lie and destroy."

Another male platypoid stood on the other side of the pool. "The only good human is a dead human."

A chorus of approval rose from the other platypus.

Pokaplatus held up her arms. "Wait! The chipmunk says this one is different."

The male pointed at Dirk. "Kill him."

Dirk scanned the crowd. With his enhanced strength and reflexes, and the integrated weapons in his wrists, he could cut through the rope and take the platypoid girls behind him, but the mob would beat him eventually. If they decided to attack, he would have to knock down the two girls and run into the jungle, then hope to outrun them. If he could get close enough to the mine, he could call in the drones to help. But then Bastado wouldn't think twice about bombing them.

"I do not trust humans," Pokaplatus said, "but the chipmunk trusts this one, and I trust her. We should listen to what he has to say. We can kill him later, if we do not agree."

The male turned and began to walk away. "I will not stay to listen to human lies."

"This is important."

The male glared at her. "When we are mated, you will learn to obey your betters."

The platypoid mob laughed.

"You are only here because you ran when the humans came," Pokaplatus said. "My own father died in the grinding machines while you hid in a lake."

He walked away. A dozen of the other males stood and shook their heads, then followed him.

"No-one has to die," Dirk said. "You just have to come to an agreement with Bastado about where he digs, and stop your attacks on the mine. Then we can work this out without anyone getting hurt."

A grey-furred platypoid stood and pointed a spear at Dirk. "There will be no agreement. Humans will not kill our sacred trees and steal our sacred soil. We will kill them all."

"As long as you say that, there can only be war. And the war will end when you are all dead."

The platypoid waved the spear above his head, and turned toward his neighbours. "There is glory in death protecting our land. There is glory in killing humans. There is no glory in skulking in a lake while humans destroy the world that gave us life."

As an ex-Space Marine, Dirk understood a desire for glory in war. But the platypoid was also insane, and he would just get them killed. "You will all die. There is no other outcome if you persist in your attacks."

The platypoid pointed the spear at Dirk. "Then let us begin by killing this one, and welcome our deaths."

"Wait," Pokaplatus said.

The other platypoids stood and stamped their paws on the rocks. "Kill the human," they chanted.

Dirk heard footsteps behind him. He glanced back. and saw two male platypoids with spears push the girls aside.

"I am your leader," Pokaplatus shouted. "You will do as I say."

The old platypoid laughed. "You are no more a leader than your useless brother. Your father left his best seed in the river when he mated your mother."

The other platypoids approached Dirk. He raised his arms, readied his integrated weapons, and hoped they would still work when he hadn't used them since leaving the Marines. He wished he knew where the platypoids had left his gauss rifle, but it was probably back at the stream with the power armour.

He glanced around him. The girls were arguing with the male platypoids who stood behind him, but at least a dozen more were coming his way. Could he jump into the pool and swim to safety? Platypoids must swim even faster than he could. He would take the spears from the first couple, then use them to hold off the others while he retreated into the jungle, then he could try to get away.

They stepped closer, their claws scraping against the wet rocks. Dirk breathed deeply and imagined happy fluffy bunnies approaching him with flowers in their teeth, rather than pointy sticks. He felt the chi power growing in his bones, but nothing that would allow him to fight a dozen at once.

"Go human," Pokaplatus said. Her whiskers dipped as she looked at him. "I will not allow them to kill you."

"Don't worry about me, I can take them," Dirk said.

"And I will not allow you to kill them, either."

She stepped between him and the approaching platypoid horde. Dirk looked over his shoulder. The two platypoid girls pushed out their chests and jiggled their bodies in front of the males. At least he didn't have to worry about an attack from that direction.

"Stop," Pokaplatus said.

The old male pushed her out of the way and raised his spear. "I will kill this human, then I will lead you to the mine, and we will die a glorious death."

He raised his spear above his shoulder. Dirk prepared to parry it with his arms. He would pull it away, swing it around, smack the platypoid on the head, then run for the jungle. He focused himself on the task ahead, where a split second would make the difference between life and death.

The male swung his spear. Then he screamed. His fur caught fire and flames rose from his body. A burned pork smell filled Dirk's lungs, and reminded him that he hadn't eaten for hours.

The platypoid's eyes opened wide as the flames grew across his fur. Then he opened his bill for a moment and fell to the rocks, before slipping off them into the pool.

Other platypoids turned and pointed spears at the sky before catching fire. The smarter ones jumped into the pool, but tall spouts of water rose around them. Dirk looked up and shaded his eyes from the sun. Drones flitted across the sky, their lasers igniting the platypoids who had not taken flight, and their bombs falling into the pool around those who were trying to swim away.

Dirk raised his arms and waved at the nearest drone as he tried to raise a wireless connection to it. Nothing.

"Stop firing," he shouted. The drone hovered and turned until its laser pointed directly at him.

"Tell Bastado to stop this," he shouted.

The drone continued to point at him. Dirk's enhanced heart beat faster, and his finely-tuned combat sense told him he should move. He dove to the rock just as the laser opened fire, melting the spot where he had stood. It had deliberately tried to hit him.

Dirk raised his arm and pointed his wrist toward the drone, exposing the integrated laser from his Space Marine days. He willed it to fire, and hoped that it still worked. The beam cut into the drone as its own laser melted rock around him. He sliced it in two, and the parts splashed down into the pool.

Pokaplatus looked at her people as they died. Another drone stopped in mid-air and turned toward her. Dirk fired at it, and it dodged behind a tree.

"Come on," Dirk said and grabbed Pokaplatus' paw. He pulled her aside just in time, as a laser melted a track across the rock where she had stood. The drone turned toward her again. Then toward him. He ducked as the laser burned through the air above his head, igniting the tail of a male platypoid behind them.

He dragged Pokaplatus toward the jungle, and shouted to the girls to run.

"I should never have listened to a human. I am so stupid."

Pokaplatus sat on a fallen tree trunk in the jungle. Dirk stood beside her, peered between, the trees and hoped no platypoids with murder on their mind were heading his way.

"Now I shall join my father in the grinding machines," she said.

Dirk sat and put his arm around her shoulder. His fingers dangled enticingly close to her furry cleavage.

"You are not going to die."

She turned her head and looked at him. He stared into her large dark brown eyes. Her bill opened slightly, and she leaned toward him. He pursed his lips and wondered whether she had a tongue.

Then she yelled, lunged forward and swung her paw toward his face with her claws outstretched. Dirk released her and dodged back, fell from the tree trunk and rolled on the muddy ground behind it. He jumped to his feet just as she threw herself at him, her bill open wide and claws swinging. He dodged again, and she fell to the ground beside him and slid to a stop on the mud.

"What the hell are you doing?" Dirk said as she tried to climb to her knees. Her paws and knees slid on the mud as she tried to get a grip, then her claws dug into the ground.

She grabbed the nearest tree and pulled herself up until she could stand. "Killing you, as I should have done when I had the chance. My people would still be alive, if you had not brought humans to them."

She held out her claws. Her fur was coated with mud, and stuck tightly to her skin. Dirk tried to put the image of a Floozie vs Pokaplatus mud-wrestling contest out of his mind as she circled him and swung the claws at his chest.

Dirk held up his hands. "I don't want to hurt you, I want to help. Bastado is an asshole."

"You lead his machines to us."

"He must have tracked me to your meeting."

She lunged at him again. Dirk tried to dodge, but his foot slipped on the mud. Her claws tore through his shirt, and scraped across his muscular chest.

"He didn't just try to kill you," Dirk said. "He tried to kill me. I'm not going to hand you over to him."

Pokaplatus stared into his eyes and breathed hard. She was preparing to attack him again. The Delhi Llama had told him real men don't hit girls, but he'd never seen this one.

She jumped forward. Dirk grabbed her and knocked her to the ground, then straddled her waist and held her arms above her head. She struggled, and tried to throw him off.

A screeching noise floated through the jungle toward them. More screeching answered it from the opposite direction.

Dirk looked at the trees, then at Pokaplatus. "What is that?"

"That is what remains of my people. They are preparing to attack the mine."

"That's crazy. Bastado will kill them all."

"They would rather die than watch him destroy our planet."

"I can't let them do that."

"You cannot stop them. If you try, they will kill you, as you deserve."

Something swished between the leaves to the right. Dirk swung his wrist laser toward it. The leaves parted and the two platypoid girls stepped through the gap. One held her arm, her skin red where a laser had burned through the fur. They looked at Dirk and Pokaplatus, then giggled.

Dirk looked into Pokaplatus's eyes.

"I have a plan. I know how you can beat Bastado."

"You would really fight your own people?"

"They tried to kill me. Besides, they're only here for tax-free wages and free beer. They'll run screaming like little girls when they realize they're losing the fight. No-one has to get hurt if we do this right."

Pokaplatus glared at him for a moment, then nodded. "If you lie, I will kill you."

Dirk climbed off her and helped her to her feet. He looked at his comrades. Pokaplatus' bosom heaved, and the maidens giggled.

Three bikini-clad furry girls and him against the world. Just the way he liked it.

Dirk and the girls strode through the jungle. Dirk had powered down his skulltop computer so Bastado couldn't track him. The injured girl leaned against him, and he put his arm around her. She tapped her tail against his ass. If she kept it up, Dirk didn't think she would be a maiden in the morning.

Pokaplatus crouched and held up her hand. "Stop."

"What is it?" Dirk said.

She pointed ahead of them at a box attached to a nearby tree at the end of a cable. "There are metal spies here."

Dirk sniggered. "Don't worry."

He strode past her and pulled the cable from the tree. It snapped, and the camera fell to the ground, smashing on a thick tree root. The casing was rusted, and a furry nose poked out of a nest of twigs and leaves inside it.

"Bastado's been cutting costs again. I brought us in this way because I knew these sensors were out of action. No-one will spot us here."

Dirk lead the way to tree line, and scanned the devastated plain of dirt and rocks beyond. The Destructobots ground their way through the undergrowth, and trees creaked and crunched as their bulldozer blades pushed against the trunks of the larger trees, while their arms ripped the smaller ones out of the ground. Something exploded, and a cloud of smoke rose above the trees opposite.

The girls pressed against Dirk. He put his arms around their waists and looked at them in turn.

"Now, girls, you have a very important part in this plan."

They giggled.

"I need you to find the other platypoids, and tell them to stop attacking the Destructobots, then find a safe place out of the way and wait for us."

"You mean the big shiny things?" the injured girl said.

Dirk nodded.

"Stop attacking them?" Pokaplatus said.

"We don't want to destroy them, we want to use them. If the platypoids can get on board and find the manual controls, they can use them against the mine. Only Bastado's heavy weapons can stop them."

"How will they do that?"

"Just wait 'til they stop moving. Now, get going."

"I want to stay with you," the injured girl said.

"I'll see you when this is over. Let's save your people and send Bastado packing."

The girls nodded and strode away into the jungle. Dirk lead Pokaplatus toward a nearby tree. It towered a hundred meters above him, and long creepers dangled from the branches. He grabbed a creeper and began to climb.

"Platypoids don't climb," Pokaplatus said.

Dirk clung to the creeper. "Time to learn."

He nodded to his left, where a loud crunching noise filled the air. A smaller robot rolled toward them on wide tracks with a large hopper of crushed rocks on the back.

"See the Minerbot? The hopper is almost full, and it's about to return to the *Pooper-Scooper*. It has cameras on the front and sides, but nothing looking up. If we can swing into the hopper, we can get to the ship without anyone seeing us."

He held out his hand. Pokaplatus wrapped her arms around her chest. If she had lips, he was sure she would be pouting.

"Come on," he said. "Do this and you'll be a hero to your people. And the ones who are still alive now won't be dead."

"I will be dead if I try to climb up there."

Dirk looked toward the Minerbot. It was almost at the tree and would pass it soon. They only had a short time to climb if they were going to get into the hopper, and if they weren't above it when it passed, the cameras might spot them.

"Stay here, then," he said. "I'll save your people myself."

He began to climb the creeper.

"Stop," Pokaplatus said.

He held out his hand and she grabbed it. He pulled her up to the creeper. The Minerbot was passing the tree.

"Let's go," he said and climbed as fast as he could. Pokaplatus followed slowly behind.

Dirk reached the first high branch above the Minerbot's hopper. He looked down, but Pokaplatus was still well below.

"Hurry up."

She looked up and glared at him, but kept climbing. The Minerbot had almost passed the tree, and she only had a few seconds. He tried to grab her arm to help her up but she was too far below. The Minerbot rolled on.

She climbed higher. Dirk grabbed her hand and pulled her to him. She looked down at the Minerbot. "We missed it."

Dirk looked at the creeper, then at the Minerbot. It looked long enough.

"Hang on," he said, and grabbed Pokaplatus by her waist. Then he held the creeper tightly with his other mechanically augmented arm, and jumped.

Pokaplatus screamed as they swung away from the tree. They passed over the Minerbot, then, as the creeper swung back, Dirk let go. He fell into the hopper on his back, and the impact knocked the breath from his lungs. Pokaplatus landed on his chest.

He breathed deeply as his body repair systems dulled the pain. Then he looked up into Pokaplatus' eyes as she lay on top of him, her legs straddling his and her breasts squashed against his chest. He put his arms around her back.

"You know, we have fifteen minutes before this thing gets to the *Pooper-Scooper*..."

Pokaplatus raised her claws and hissed.

The Minerbot rolled into the *Pooper-Scooper*'s mining bays. Men and machines worked around them, unloading the hopper of a Minerbot that was already in a bay. Others were processing the dirt and rocks they pulled out.

Dirk peered over the edge of the hopper. Pokaplatus knelt beside him, but Dirk pushed her down when she tried to look past.

"What are you doing?" Pokaplatus said.

"If they see me, they might still think I'm on their side. They won't think the same about you."

The Minerbot slowed, turned and stopped at an empty bay. Dirk pointed to the gantry above them.

"We're going that way."

He helped Pokaplatus up, then lifted her foot in his hands so she could reach the gantry. As she climbed, she smacked him in the face with her tail.

He climbed up behind her. The gantry was small, but high enough above the bay floor that the guards and workers below were unlikely to see them. He pointed to where it reached the wall, and they crawled along it to the end. Dirk stayed a safe distance behind Pokaplatus' tail and kept an eye on the people below, but none appeared to have any curiosity about what might be happening above them.

"Now what?" Pokaplatus said.

Dirk pointed toward a door below. "We need to get into the ship, then find our way to the reactor room."

Before he could say anything else, Pokaplatus swung her legs over the side of the gantry and pushed off. She dropped to the gantry below them, which rattled with the impact.

One of the engineers looked up. Pokaplatus crouched low behind the railing. The engineer muttered something to the man alongside, and they both peered at the wall.

Dirk waited and watched. The men muttered something again, then turned away.

Dirk slid from the side of the gantry, and hung onto the edge as he lowered himself as far as possible. He dropped the last couple of feet onto the lower gantry, then lay prone so the people below wouldn't see him. He waved at Pokaplatus and motioned for her to creep toward the door.

As they reached it, Dirk looked over the railing. The men who had been looking at them before were climbing the steps at the far end of the gantry. In a moment they would turn the corner, then they would be able to see right along it. That would leave no chance of hiding, and little chance of fighting their way out if they managed to call for help.

Dirk crouched by the door and tried to pull it open.

The gantry rattled as the men walked along it.

"Hurry," Pokaplatus said.

"I'd kind of hoped that someone would have left the door open. The only other way in is to use my access code, and that will warn them that we're here anyway."

Pokaplatus looked along the gantry and extended her claws. "I will not be taken alive. Some of these scum will die with me."

The rattling grew louder as the men approached the corner. Dirk tried to push his enhanced fingers into the rubber seal around the door, so he could get enough of a grip to try to pull it open. But they only found metal beyond.

"Let's hope it doesn't come to that," he said. He lay on the gantry, and aimed his wrist laser toward the far end.

The door opened. Dirk rolled, and pushed himself to a crouch, aiming the laser at the door. They weren't going to catch him without a fight.

A familiar furry face peered out at them.

"Floozie," Dirk said. "What are you doing here?"

"I saw you on the surveillance cameras. It's lucky everyone else is too lazy to watch them. Now get in here."

She pushed the door wide open, and Dirk and Pokaplatus hurried in. Floozie closed it behind them.

"Still wearing your bikini?" Dirk said.

"Bastado wanted me to wear it."

Dirk could understand that in generalities, but still wasn't quite sure of the specifics.

"Why?"

Floozie sighed, and crossed her arms. "He wanted me to pretend to be a platypoid princess, so he could tie me up and spank me."

Pokaplatus scowled. "I will kill that man."

"Join the queue," Dirk said. He turned to Floozie. "The platypoids are attacking. Bastado is going to kill them if we don't do something."

"So what are we going to do?" Floozie said.

"We need to get to the reactor somehow," Dirk said, and nodded toward Pokaplatus. "Maybe I could pretend she's my prisoner."

Floozie shook her head, then stared up at him. "And you're taking her to the reactor room. Totally makes sense."

"I'll think of something."

"Bastado is waiting for me. I have to go."

Dirk nodded. "Keep him busy."

Floozie rolled her eyes. "What do you think I've been doing for the last month?"

Dirk opened the door, and stepped into the reactor room. Two engineers sat at the consoles and looked up at him. The tall one's nameplate said Locke, the other Callahan. Dirk was glad to see that his expectation was correct, and they weren't armed. He covered the slashes in his shirt with his hand.

"Hi," he said. "Security check."

Locke picked up a clipboard and flipped through it, while Callahan stared at Dirk.

"So how's it going?" Dirk said. "I heard the platypoids are attacking, and wanted to make sure everything was okay down here. This reactor is important to our security."

Locke slapped the clipboard down on the console. "You're not the security chief any more. Mr Bastado said the platypoids killed you."

Dirk laughed. "That was another security test. Mr Bastado would tell you I was dead, then I'd come down and see whether you questioned me. Well done, you've passed."

He held out his free hand to Callahan, who shook it. Then he held it out to the Locke.

Locke ignored him, flipped through his clipboard again, then began pressing buttons on the console. "This isn't right. I'm checking with Mr Bastado."

"No need to do that," Dirk said.

Locke looked at him. "I thought you said we were supposed to question you?" He pressed another button, and Floozie's voice came from a nearby speaker.

"Oh, I've been such a naughty princess. Spank me, master. I deserve it."

"What if I like my princess naughty?" Bastado's voice said.

"Spank her, and she'll be twice as naughty."

Something slapped, and Floozie squealed.

Locke blushed as he looked at the console screen. "Excuse me, sir..."

"What the hell do you think you're doing?" Bastado said. "Can't you see I'm busy?"

"Yes, sir, but..."

"Get off the line."

Locke began to open his mouth again, looked at Dirk, then closed it. Floozie squealed, and Locke pressed another button that shut off the sound.

"See," Dirk said. "Mr Bastado wouldn't be playing *Spank The Naughty Princess* if I was really a threat."

A cooling pressure warning light flashed on the console, and Locke glanced down at it. Dirk coughed and stepped forward, then nodded toward the door at the back of the room. "Now, open the door, so I can check the reactor."

Locke stood and blocked the path to the door. "No-one goes in there without Mr Bastado's permission."

Dirk smiled. "That's a shame."

Locke's eyes narrowed as they stared into Dirk's. No matter, his diversion had worked. Pokaplatus should have reached the reactor through the cooling water pipes, and would be ready to cause havoc.

Alarms rang, and more lights flashed on the consoles.

"You see," Dirk said. "If you'd let me in, I might have been able to stop the platypoid attack."

"Grab him," Locke said, and motioned to the Callahan, who shook his head. Locke punched buttons on the console. Floozie's squeals filled the room again.

"Mr Bastado," he said.

Then the power went out.

Dirk punched Locke, and he slumped down in his chair. The lights flickered back on, and Callahan watched in silence. Dirk punched him for good measure.

More warning lights flashed.

"Something's in the intake vents," Callahan spluttered.

"What do you mean?" Dirk said.

His heart jumped a beat. Pokaplatus shouldn't have gone that far. He told her to stay away from the vents, so she wouldn't be sucked in.

Callahan pointed to one of the displays. "It's going to be sucked into the turbines."

Dirk leaned over the console. What could he do to stop it? He punched buttons at random in the hope that he could find something to save her.

Then a shriek of tearing metal filled the room, the turbines went red on the display, and the power went out for good.

Dirk looked at the screen in silence as it flickered, then emergency lights illuminated the room. "Oh shit."

He pushed past the engineers, and through the door. He stepped out onto the gantry and leaned over the side. Water swirled on the level below where the pipes had broken apart.

"Pokaplatus!" he shouted.

Dirk heard footsteps on the gantry and glanced behind him. Locke raced toward him, with hands outstretched. Dirk raised his hand to defend himself, then Locke screamed and flew past him over the railing. He bounced from the wall and splashed into the water below.

Pokaplatus climbed over the railing, her fur soaked. She rubbed her paws together and laughed. "Should look below him."

Dirk looked down at the water. Locke floated back to the surface and began to doggy-paddle around the room. "I thought..."

"After I pulled some cables free I thought I should push them into the vents." She looked at Dirk. "I did good?"

Dirk nodded. "For now. They won't get this working again for a while."

Callahan looked at them, then turned and ran back to the control room.

"Let us find Bastado," Pokaplatus said.

Dirk trudged up the stairs behind Pokaplatus.

"Next time, let's destroy the ship's reactor after we take the elevator to the bad guy's lair. Or, at least, pick one who lives underground so it's all downhill."

Dirk heard footsteps up ahead, which rapidly grew louder. He stepped past Pokaplatus, and pushed her into a doorway.

A red face appeared, then more behind it as a dozen of the engineers trotted down the stairs, carrying bags of tortilla chips and kegs of beer.

"Come on, mate," Blair said. "We're getting out of here."

Dirk leaned across the doorway, hiding Pokaplatus behind him. "I have to see Bastado."

"Suit yourself. Those fur-bags have stolen the Destructobots. We're taking the shuttle, and it won't be waiting for stragglers."

The mob of engineers strode past, puffing and panting as they hurried down the steps. As the noise faded, Dirk stepped out and peered through the nearby window. The Destructobots were moving away from the trees and approaching the ship. With the reactor shut down, the mining computer had switched to safe mode and released control of them.

Then one of the Destructobots turned sideways, and drove across the path of another. The second Destructobot smacked into the side of the first and sent it spinning, then pushed it up onto one track and over on its side. The second Destructobot rode up over it and stopped, one track hanging in the air.

Platypoids climbed from the Destructobot that lay on its side, and waved their spears at the others. In a moment the crews of both Destructobots were hitting the other with the butt of their spears.

Dirk shook his head. Then a third Destructobot smashed into the crashed two and sent them and the platypoids flying.

"They won't have to worry about guards," Pokaplatus said. "They are more dangerous to themselves."

"Let's just hope they can distract everyone until we get to Bastado."

They climbed the tower stairs as fast as they could. Dirk's augmented legs took them two steps at a time, but he had to wait for Pokaplatus to catch up. They were almost at Bastado's office when muffled shouts echoed around the stairwell.

Dirk rushed to the top of the stairs, and kicked open the door. The action froze inside the room as he stared in. Floozie was backing away from Bastado as he rode his chair around the office. The lizard clung to Floozie's hair, and flicked its tongue at Dirk. Floozie held a potted palm high above her head, as though ready to hit Bastado with it.

Pokaplatus stepped up beside Dirk. She looked at Bastado, raised her paws and extended her claws.

"Spank me, would you?" she said.

"Oh crap," Bastado said.

Gunfire rattled outside the ship. Dirk glanced through the window. Most of the Destructobots were crashed and burning in the distance, and the platypoids were fighting each other around them. But one Destructobot was rolling toward them, gauss rifle rounds ricocheting off the blade and hull.

"Give it up, Bastado," Dirk said. "You've lost."

"Let me kill him," Pokaplatus said.

Dirk put his arm out and held her back. "No. Give him a chance to surrender."

"Good. After he surrenders, he will face the *Death of a Thousand Claws*."

Dirk hadn't intended to kill Bastado, but when he thought back to the flaming platypoids, young and old, male and female, screaming as they dove into the water to try to put out the flames in their fur, he began to reconsider. Yet for all his murderous plans, the man seemed harmless now.

Bastado turned his chair toward Dirk and scowled. Floozie shouted, and Dirk ducked just as flames erupted from one arm of the chair. Bullets cracked past his head and exploded on the wall behind him, spraying fragments of metal and plastic into the air.

Pokaplatus jumped toward Bastado, who turned the chair and fired again. The explosive rounds tore into Floozie's desk and Pokaplatus ducked behind it.

Dirk fired his laser. It burned through the side of the chair arm, and sparks flew from the chair as the heat ignited several rounds inside it. They exploded, and blew out the side of the chair. It twisted and tilted sideways as the anti-grav field bent.

"Fuck," Bastado said, as he slapped hot shrapnel fragments away from his bare thighs.

"Give up," Dirk said, and aimed his laser at Bastado's face.

"No. You give up, or the chipmunk gets it."

Dirk glanced at Floozie. The lizard had wrapped its tail around her neck, and its long tongue flicked at her face.

"The Reticulan Slime Lizard can kill with one bite," Bastado said. "Such a death is neither pretty nor painless, and I'm sure you do not want to see an innocent bystander killed just so you can capture me."

Dirk glanced at Pokaplatus. She was crawling behind the desk toward Bastado.

Bastado laughed. "You didn't think I kept it around for company, did you?"

"Harm her and you will die the death of... the worst thing I can come up with at the time. And I saw some unimaginably horrible ways to die when I was in the Space Marines."

"I think we have a stand-off."

Dirk heard grinding outside, and glanced out through the window. The guards were climbing aboard the engineers' shuttle, and the remaining Destructobot was roaring toward the ship, crushing parked drones beneath its tracks.

"Perhaps not."

Bastado followed Dirk's gaze. His knuckles grew white as his hands tightened on the arm of his chair. Pokaplatus climbed over the desk and jumped toward him.

The Destructobot slammed into the side of the ship. Metal creaked and cracked below them, the walls shook, and the floor tilted. Dirk and Pokaplatus fell, and the lizard screeched as it slipped from Floozie's shoulder and flew across the room. Floozie slid sideways, and smacked into Bastado's chair.

"I shall need this one for company," Bastado said. He grabbed her arm and pulled her toward him.

"No," Floozie shouted, and smacked Bastado's hand. He grabbed her around the waist, and his chair backed away.

Floozie swung her elbow. It smacked Bastado's nose with a loud crunch of breaking bone. He yelled in pain, and released her.

Pokaplatus lunged for his chair. Bastado spun the chair around and raced for the office door, knocking her away in the process. Dirk raised his wrist laser and fired, but he was too late. The door slammed shut, and Dirk's laser beam just burned a scorch-mark on the wood.

"Let's get him," Dirk said. Pokaplatus was already at the door, scratching her claws on the wood. Dirk grabbed the handle and tried to twist it. It was stuck.

"No," Floozie said as the room began to shake. "His office is a lifeboat. He's going to run before we can do anything."

Dirk imagined Bastado's office blasting into space, escaping whatever fate he might deserve. Then he imagined the rocket exhaust blasting into the antechamber where they stood. The shaking grew louder, the lifeboat would launch within seconds.

"Let's go," he said.

"I will kill him," Pokaplatus said.

"He'll kill you if we don't get out of here now. If you're alive, there's another chance."

Floozie was already running toward the stairs. Pokaplatus looked at Dirk as a loud whine filled the room. He grabbed her hand and pulled her toward the stairs.

They raced down the stairs, taking them four at a time. Floozie stopped on the landing below, and hit the emergency exit release by the window. It blew outward, and an escape slide inflated. She glanced back at Dirk and Pokaplatus, then jumped. Dirk followed her down the slide, Pokaplatus whooping behind him, then they slid to a halt on the bare dirt outside the ship.

They lay on the ground as the roar of the lifeboat's exhaust filled their ears and flames belched out of the emergency exit, setting the slide alight. The lifeboat rose into the sky on a column of flame, then disappeared behind the clouds.

Dirk heard grinding and looked behind him. The remaining Destructobot slid to a halt. The cabin doors clicked open and lifted up.

The two platypoid maidens peered out, waved, and giggled.

"Do you think the platypoids are safe now?" Floozie said.

Dirk put his arm around her shoulder. "I think Bastado will be back in a month with a pack of mercenaries and a stack of Nova bombs. If we can prove he got the mining permit through fraud, we can still stop him. If not, we have time to convince the platypoids to move away from here."

"I just wish we could do more."

"You can't win them all," Dirk said. He turned her around and pulled her to him, squashing her breasts against his chest. He looked down at the cleavage. "Is that bikini the only thing you have to wear?"

She nodded. "The rest of my clothes were in Bastado's closet, which is now heading for deep space."

Dirk smiled at her. "I hoped you were going to say that."

Someone coughed. Dirk looked around. Pokaplatus stood in the water nearby, looking at them. She chirped.

"Human, I wish to offer you the honour of mating with me."

Floozie growled deep in her throat. Dirk studied Pokaplatus' breasts as they bulged out of her torn bikini, then felt Floozie's hand slide into his pants. He looked down at her.

"Remember, I have claws," she whispered.

"For us to mate," Pokaplatus said, "would be to indicate a lasting friendship between platypoid-kind and the best of the humans."

Dirk leaned his head toward Floozie's. Which wasn't easy, because she was two feet shorter than him. "If I don't, there could be an interplanetary incident. I couldn't live with that on my conscience."

Floozie growled, pulled her hand from his pants, then slid out of his grasp. She sat on a rock by the water and lounged provocatively. Dirk hoped that, when Bambi turned up next week, she wasn't going to object to a threesome.

Pokaplatus walked toward him, then took his hand and pulled him into the water. She chirped again.

"In the water?" Dirk said.

"When two tribes wish to make an alliance, it is tradition to show respect by a Prince of one tribe mating with a maiden Princess, in front of the entire tribe. After he is done, any other maiden present may demand her right to mate with him too."

The platypoid maidens giggled and held up their hands.

Pokaplatus looked at Floozie. "You may join the audience if you wish."

Floozie leaned on her elbow. "That does sound like a sight worth seeing." She smiled at Dirk. "I'm sure it would make an interesting recording for anthropological study."

Dirk looked at Floozie, then at Pokaplatus. "And if I can't satisfy their demands?"

Pokaplatus hissed. "That would be an unimaginable insult to my people and death for you. Many terrible wars have been fought because a Prince could not perform his Royal duty."

Dirk looked at the fast-flowing water, then at the maidens preening themselves, then at Pokaplatus, whose breasts bulged around her neck like a life jacket as she trod water.

"This could be hard."

"It is a test of courage and stamina. Dirk Beretta has already proven that he has plenty of both."

Dirk smiled. "I guess I have."

ABOUT THE AUTHOR

Edward M. Grant spent his childhood in the South-West of Britain and studied Physics at Oxford, but now lives in Canada. He wrote magazine articles and worked on numerous indie movies in and around London, including co-writing a vampire movie that was later shot in California. He has travelled the world, been a VIP at several space shuttle launches, survived earthquakes and a tsunami, climbed Mt Fuji and visits nuclear explosion sites as a hobby.

He grew up on pulp horror and SF novels and still has a soft spot for both. However, his background as a physicist helps him write stories toward the harder end of the SF spectrum.

Find him online at **www.edwardmgrant.com,** *or subscribe to his new release mailing list at* **www.edwardmgrant.com/list.**

AUTHOR'S NOTES

Dirk Beretta was a character I invented some years ago in a writing example for a web forum, but somehow he just seemed to stick. I liked the idea of the tough, but not terribly smart, ex-space marine who had been inducted in some wacky religion by a crazy cult leader.

A version of this story was originally published under a pen-name. When I first released it I thought I should keep the funny SF stories separate to the more serious stories I've been writing under this name, but I later decided I should really keep them all together. So I've tweaked and edited the original versions and I'm re-releasing them under my name.

ALSO BY EDWARD M. GRANT

SPACE WEASELS

Vicious, congenitally bureaucratic, and proud of their resplendent flame-red uniforms which give them a five minute life expectancy in combat, the Flaming Space Weasels wiped out most of Dirk Beretta's fellow space marines at the battle of Din Bin Foo... then served them for lunch with a nice Merlot.

In the aftermath, Dirk quits his job as poster boy for the space marines, to drown his sorrow in cheap booze and cheaper women. But when a gang of pirate Weasels come hunting fresh meat for the kibble factories, his brand of pig-headed determination and excessive violence may offer the chance for redemption... and revenge.

A 7,000 word science fiction short story.

DEATH TO DEMOCRACY

After Dirk Beretta saves the Winterbotham Nachos heiress from a fate worse than death in the Space Weasel kibble factories, a romantic cruise around the galaxy with her looks like a well-earned rest.

But Royalist revolutionaries on the Planet Of The Squid have other ideas. When they hatch a plan to replace the democratic government with moronic monarchy, Dirk Beretta faces a difficult choice: can he kill his new drinking buddy to save democracy?

A 9,000 word science fiction short story.